THE CHOSEN ONES OF EGYPT

THE CHOSEN ONES OF EGYPT

LINDI HAMLIN

iUniverse, Inc.
Bloomington

The Chosen Ones of Egypt

iUniverse books may be ordered through booksellers or by contacting:

iUniverse
1663 Liberty Drive
Bloomington, IN 47403
www.iuniverse.com
1-800-Authors (1-800-288-4677)

ISBN: 978-1-4620-0558-1 (sc)
ISBN: 978-1-4620-0559-8 (ebk)

Printed in the United States of America

iUniverse rev. date: 03/14/2011

CHAPTER 1

Ace Mann was waiting on a customer. He and his twin brother Trace owes an ice cream shop. The shop is call the Twin Sweet Delights. At the Twin Sweet Delights customers can also buy candy, cupcakes and other sweet stuff. They also make special cakes such as birthdays and weddings. "I can't believe that no one on St. Simon wants to hire me!" A woman complained as she entered the shop.

"Will that be all sir?" Ace asked the customer. The man said yes and Ace rang his order up. "Thank you sir and enjoy your stay while you are here on St. Simon Island Georgia." Ace turned to the woman and asked her. "What happened to your retail job?"

"I got fired this morning." She replied.

"Why?" Ace asked.

"I got into an argument with my boss."

"You have gotten into arguments before with Mindy and she has never fired you." Ace replied.

"I guess that she did not like it when I decked her one square in the eye."

"Why did you do that?" Ace asked.

"She told me that I was too much of a bitch for you and that you will be her boyfriend and not me."

"Amanda you know that I love you. Mindy and I will never go out no matter how much she tries to get me. I only have eyes for you."

"I know that Ace but it was the way she said it." Amanda said. Ace came out from behind the counter and gave his girlfriend a hug.

1

"What is going on?" Trace asked. He had just stepped out of the office.

"Amanda just got herself fired because she decked Mindy in the eye this morning." Ace answered.

"Did you blackened her eye?" Trace asked.

"She will not be able to see out of that eye for a couple of days." Amanda answered.

"Give me a high five! It is about time that someone put that bitch in her place!" Trace said as Amanda gave him his high five.

"I am going have a hard time with coming up with my share of the rent until I can find a job." Amanda groaned.

"Celeste and Gail will understand." Ace said.

"Yes they will but it will put them in a bind to pay for my share." Amanda said.

"You are in luck because you do have a job." Trace said.

"Where?" Amanda asked.

"Here. Evelyn quite this morning." Trace answered.

"She did? Why?" Ace asked.

"She ran off with Bob Richardson to get marry." Trace replied.

"She can't do that! Bob is a married man." Ace said.

"I know that but she said that Bob will be leaving his wife for her." Trace said.

"What is the church going to do now for a preacher since Bob left?" Amanda asked.

"I don't know but the next preacher that we get better not leave his wife for another woman in the congregation." Trace said.

"I can hear it now in church Sunday morning. No one will be talking about the lord. They all will be talking about Bob especially Mrs. Green." Ace said.

"I need a double pistachio cone now!" A woman said as she approached the group.

"What happened to your diet? Celeste." Trace asked.

"After the day I just had I am going off of it." Celeste said as Ace handed her a cone.

"It sounds like that you had a bad day." Ace said.

"I did." Celeste said.

"What about the money?" Ace asked as he rang her up.

"Trace will pay for it." She replied.

"I will?' Trace asked.

"You are my boyfriend." She said.

Trace handed his brother the money. "Keep the change." Trace said.

"What change? You are shorting me by fifty cents." Ace said.

"That is all I have on me." Trace said. Ace put the fifty cents in from his own pockets.

"A patient of mine an old man who is recovering from a stroke slapped me on the butt! I told him that

I was his therapist not his lover and if he wanted to keep the use of his good arm that he will never touch me again!" Celeste fumed.

"What is everybody doing?" A blonde man asked as he entered. A police woman followed him in.

"Hi Andy! Hi Gail!" Ace said.

"Can you get me a coke?" The police officer asked.

"I thought that all police likes to hang out in the doughnut shops." Trace said as he handed her a coke.

"Not this cop." Gail said.

"Amanda got fired because she decked Mindy in the eye." Ace said.

"If you need a lawyer I can represent you because I am sure she deserved it." Andy said.

"I got fussed out today by my sergeant because I lost a bank robber suspect that I had to chase on foot. I wasn't the only officer involved but I was the only one to get fussed at. I was the only woman there and that is the reason I got fussed at." Gail said

"It sounds like you have a case. I will represent you." Andy said.

"I don't want to make a fuss." Gail said.

"I thought that you would be here Amanda. I need you back in the store." A woman said.

"You fired me today ." Amanda reminded her.

"I know that you need a job so I will let you come back."

"She doesn't need a job. She has a job here and by the way I love your black eye Mindy."

"Shut up Trace!" Mindy said through gritted teeth.

"I am not Trace. I am Ace."

"Where did Evelyn go?" Andy asked.

"She ran off to get marry to Bob Richardson." Trace replied.

"Bob is married." Celeste said.

"She said that Bob was going to divorce his wife to marry her." Trace said.

"That creep! He promised me that he would leave his wife for me!" Mindy yelled as she ran out the door.

"I guess that Bob wasn't very preacherly after all." Trace remarked. Everyone laughed.

"Living here on St.Simon is never boring." Andy said. Everyone had to agree.

"My lord, I have found the Chosen Ones." A man dressed in ancient Egyptian clothing said as he bowed down before a man dressed in ancient Egyptian pharaoh clothing.

"You may arise my child." The man in pharaoh clothing said. The other man stood up. "Who are they and where are they now?"

"Ace Mann, Trace Mann, Andy Jackson, Amanda Lea, Celeste Peavey, and Gail Able. They are all in a place call America and on StSimon Georgia.:" The man in ancient Egyptian clothing said.

"Ariole go and find them. Bring them back. We need their service again if we are going to save the world."

"Yes my lord." Ariole replied.

"Ariole don't forget that they probably do not remember who they were. You are going have to find a way to remind them."

"Yes my lord." Ariole said. as he bowed again. He then aimed his bracelet that he was wearing in the air and a hole appeared with a circle blue light around it. He then disappeared in the circle as the circle closed. He emerged from the circle on StSimon Island Georgia.

CHAPTER 2

Ariole started to walk in the direction that he thought he needed to go in. People were staring at him but he ignored them. He came to the fishing pier. "Hey dude! What kind of clothes are you wearing?" A curly hair teenage boy asked.

"What is this hey dude?" Ariole asked.

"It is an expression. You are not from this country are you?"

"No. I am from Egypt. I am also coming from a different time frame." Ariole explained.

"What kind of drugs are you on?" Ariole ignored the kid and walked away. A woman screamed. Ariole looked to see a man beating the woman who was screaming with his fist. "I told you that I wanted a beer!" The man yelled at her.

"Stanley, you are drunk! You had enough beer. I thought a coke would be better." The woman cried.

"I decide when I have had enough!" The man yelled.

"It is wrong to beat a woman." Ariole said to the man.

"Who the hell are you!" The man yelled at Ariole.

"I am just passing through." Ariole replied.

The man pulled his fist back to hit the woman again. Ariole grabbed the man's fist. "I told you that it is wrong to beat a woman!" Ariole said as he glared at the man.

"What are you going to do about it?" The man asked. Ariole pulled the man to him then he picked the man up and threw him into the water. People stood far away from Ariole because he was several yards away from the water but he had managed to pick this big man up and throw him into the water.

"Hey dude forget that I had even spoken to you." The teenage boy said as he got on his bicycle and pedaled away as fast as he could.

People started to clap as Ariole walked away. One man hollered "That is the way to show that man that he can't beat up a woman!"

Ariole turned around to face the man. "Why didn't you do something to stop it? You was closer than I was."

The man gulped and replied. "I was too scared."

"I know these people who are called the Chosen Ones. They too were afraid to stand up for what is right but they stood up together and fought for what is right. They fought all evil. They saved the world more than once. All it takes is for people to stand up and fight together for what is right." Ariole then walked off without glancing back.

"Can I help you?" Amanda asked a customer.

"You can. I want all of the money." The man said as he pulled a hand gun on her.

Amanda didn't say anything. She quickly opened the cash register. "Amanda we need to order." Ace stopped what he was going to say because he saw the man with the gun.

"You stand over by the girl." The man ordered.

"You can take all of the money just don't shoot anyone." Ace said as he carefully moved toward Amanda.

"Ace what is taking you so long? You and Amanda have better not be kissing while at work." Trace yelled as he came out of the office. He saw the man with the gun. Trace said. "I will be in the office because I am not really here."

"Stop! Get over by these two." The man stared at Trace and he glanced at Ace.

"I am only a mirror image of that man. I am not really here." Trace said.

Ace reached out an arm and pulled his brother to him. "Trace do not anger the man with the gun."

"Right because I really am here. We are twins." Trace said to the man.

"I can see that. No one move."

"Hey everyone! I mean bye everyone." Andy turned to walk out of the shop.

"You get over there by those three."

"When you get caught and you will I can get you off with less years if you don't shoot anyone. I am a lawyer so please don't shoot me. You just might need my help." Andy said as he went slowly to stand by the others.

"What is this place? This place was empty just a few minutes ago and now everyone is dropping by." The man with the gun said.

"That some times happen when you run a business. It can be slow one minute and the next minute we could have a full house." Trace smirked.

Ace hit his brother over the head. "We do not need to hear your smart mouth right now!"

"Drop the Gun!" Gail ordered as she came in in uniform with her gun drawn. There was a gun shot and Gail felled to the floor another robber came in. Amanda screamed. Celeste was out side when she heard the gun shot and Amanda screaming. She ran inside just as the robbers pushed pass her. She saw her friend laying on the floor. Andy was beside his girlfriend. He was on her radio trying to get help.

Celeste ran over to her friend and dropped down beside her. She placed Gail's head on her lap. "I am going to die." Gail said weakly.

"No you are not!" Celeste cried.

"I can feel it." Gail said before she lost conceness.

"I wish I could heal you." Celeste cried. All of a sudden a bolt of electricity went through Celeste's body. She jumped at the impact. Her hands moved over Gail's body and to the gun shot wound in her back. Blue light started to glow from Celeste's hands. The blood dried up and Gail came to.

Andy lifted up Gail's shirt and said. "Gail your shirt has a bullet hole in it but you are no longer bleeding nor is there a bullet inside of you."

Andy saw the bullet laying on the floor. He picked it up to examine it. It indeed had blood on it and it indeed had made an impact in some thing. "Celeste how did you do that?"

"I don't know." She replied.

Gail jumped up. "Where did the robber go?"

"There were two of them. They took off in a white van heading south." Celeste said. Gail ran after them.

"Gail don't you want your patrol car?" Andy called after her. "She is really running fast. She is only a blur."

"I didn't think that it was possible for anybody to run that fast." Celeste said.

"No one can." Andy said slowly.

"Guys that white van is going to collide with a group of tourists on bicycles on Oak Street. We have to stop them!" Amanda said as she ran to her car. Everyone else followed.

"Trace, you have your elbow in my stomached!" Ace complained as Amanda droved her car.

"I can't help it! It isn't my fault that Amanda drives a small car." Trace argued.

"Gail!" Amanda slammed on her brakes. Gail ran over to them.

"Get in! Amanda says that those two van is going to crash into some tourists out bicycling on Oak Street. We are going to try and stop them" Celeste said.

Gail jumped in. "How did you get this far? It should have taken you twenty minutes but it has only taken you five minutes." Andy said.

"I don't know." Gail said.

Amanda drove as fast as she could. "There they are!" She yelled. She saw the tourists on their bikes. The van was heading straight to them. Everyone jumped out of the car.

"What are we going to do? It isn't like we can move the van away from the tourists using our minds." Ace said as he waved his hand in the air. The van was pushed back and away from the tourists then the van crashed into a tree.

"I think that you just moved that van out of the way with your mind." Trace said to his brother.

The two men climbed out of the van and aimed their guns at the six friends. All of them jumped behind Amanda's car for cover. "I wish that I had their guns in my hands so they couldn't shoot us." Trace said. He screamed and dropped the two guns that had actually appeared in his hands.

"At least now they don't have guns." Andy said as he jumped up to run after the two robbers. One of the men threw a knife at him but Andy jumped high into the air. He was as high as the tallest tree when he came down he crashed into the two robbers. Gail ran up to place the cuffs on them.

"I wish I had another pair of cuffs." She said.

"Too bad that I can't say a pair of cuffs and have it appear in my hands." Trace said. He looked down at his hands as a pair of cuffs appeared. "Here." Trace said as he handed Gail the cuffs.

"How did you do that?" Ace asked his brother.

"I don't know but I am scaring myself." Trace wined.

"All of us are scaring me right now." Andy said.

Gail met everyone at the twins house. It was late at night. "What did you tell your sergeant?" Andy asked.

"I told him that I was shot but I had on my bullet proof vest and that you didn't know about it." Gail replied.

"He believed that." Andy said.

"Yes he did but I had no explanation for taking a civilian's car into the line of fire when my patrol car was capable of taking me there. I am suspended without pay for two weeks."

"That is going to make it difficult for us to pay our bills." Celeste said.

"I will pay for Gail's part." Andy volunteered.

"Andy you do not have to do that." Gail said.

"I am a lawyer. I can give you the money. It isn't going to hurt me. I am also your boyfriend that means you can count on me to help you when you need help." Andy said.

"I don't see how I can move things with my mind." Ace said frustrated. He waved his hand and his friends were thrown against the wall.

"Be careful! Your hand is a deadly weapon right now!" Trace said.

"Sorry. I also can't understand why you Trace can all of a sudden pull things out of thin air or how Andy can now levitate up to the tallest tree and come down on the robbers or how Amanda is all of a sudden a physic and how Gail can out run the road runner or how Celeste can heal Gail. We all know that Gail was shot but some how Celeste was able to heal her."

"I can answer those questions for you." A man said. He had materialized in the livening room.

"Who are you and where did you come from?" Ace demanded.

"I am Ariole and I come from ancient Egypt." He smiled at the six friends.

CHAPTER 3

"How can we be the Chosen Ones?" Ace asked.

"It makes no sense." Trace agreed.

"If we were the Chosen Ones in a previous life than we should remember something." Andy said.

"Most of the time we do not remember our past lives." Amanda said.

"Amanda, you can't really believe in that crap and you can't really believe this man? He is a freak. He belongs in a nut house." Ace pointed to Ariole.

"I don't know what to believe but I do believe in the unknown. There are things that happens in this World that we can't explain." Amanda confessed.

"Okay, you are right there are some things that can't be explained but I can assure you that this man is Crazy." Ace pointed to Ariole again.

"Will you please stop pointing at me. It isn't nice to point." Ariole said.

"I for one do not believe. I am a lawyer. I need proof to believe." Andy said.

"How do you explain the fact that you can levitate yourself? How can you explain that Ace can move Objects with his mind and Trace can make things appear in thin air or how I can predict the future. How can Gail run faster than a speeding bullet and how can Celeste heal us?" Amanda asked.

"Alright you prooved your point." Andy said a little miffed.

"What were our names when we lived in ancient Egypt?" Gail asked Ariole.

"Names are not important. What is important is saving the world and you six are the only ones who can Do that." Ariole said.

"I would still like to know who we all were." Gail insisted.

Ariole told them but he did not speak English instead he spoke Egyptian. "How is it that I can understand You?" Ace asked.

"You all can understand me because you all lived as Egyptians one time of your lives." Ariole explained.

"But we couldn't understand Egyptian before." Ace argued.

"That is because I wasn't with you but I am now so you can understand." Ariole said.

"Explain to me again just who the Chosen Ones really are and what are we up against?" Ace asked.,

"The Chosen Ones are a team of crusaders made up of six people. Crusaders are mortals with special Powers. The powers were given to crusaders to aid in the fight against evil such as demons. Every crusaders Has a protector to protect them. Protectors are classified as the nonliving which simply means that we were Once living beings but we are now dead. We do keep our physical bodies."

Ariole continued to explain. "Maku, the demon that you are up against was actually a god but he got Greedy and tried to over throw the other gods but he was beaten and cast out. Maku rebelled from the under World by uniting the demons. He also found mortals who were willingly to help him. The mortal had to give Him their souls. The mortals thought they would have ever lasting life but of coarse they didn't. All mortals Do die and Maku's mortals when they died were trapped in the world and no one could see them. They Couldn't do harm to the living accept when they were able to get back into their bodies. These are the Undead. The bodies decays after time so we have what you all would call zombies. The undead learned how To posses inanimate objects when their bodies finally decayed completely."

"What happened to Maku?" Ace asked.

"The Chosen Ones defeated him with the Charu which is a bracelet and the charu have been found by a Modern person that is how Maku was released. The charu has to be found in order to defeat Maku. You will have to trap Maku in the charu by using the caru which is like a key to the charu. All you have to Do is say a chant and point the charu at him. He will be sucked back into the charu and the caru will lock the Charu both will have to be buried. The charu and the caru must never be separated for if they are then the Living dead will arise. Maku doesn't have his full power right now. He will try to obtain it at the city of the Dead,. He will have to have the crystal triangle which is in a pyramid. Once he obtains the crystal triangle he Will have his full power."

"Will the living dead greet us when we arrive?" Trace asked.

"Only if the charu and the caru are separated." Ariole replied.

"Are we going have to travel back in time?" Ace asked Ariole.

"Yes." Ariole answered.

"We are going to do this then." Andy stated,.

"If we don't do this then the world will be destroyed." Ace replied.

"Just what I always wanted to do save the world." Andy said.

"Amanda will lead you to the charu and the caru. She can pick up the vibrations physically. I need to Warn you that whoever the charu decides to choose that person will die in seven days if the mission is not Completed within that amount of time." Ariole said.

"There is always a catch." Andy stated.

"Maku knows that you all exist he will be expecting you so be careful. You all have swords. All you have to do to get your swords is just visualized them and the swords will appear." Ariole advised.

Celeste looked down on her wrist and she saw a tattoo of star inside a triangle that was inside a hexagon "Look" She shown the others who also had the same tattoo.

"That is the mark of the Chosen Ones for as long as you are the Chosen Ones you will always have that Tattoo." Ariole said,.

"What are we waiting for? We have a charu and a caru to find." Ace said.

CHAPTER 4

"Amanda, here is a globe. See if you can find where the charu and the caru are at." Ace instructed There was a knock at the door and Trace walked over to answer since they were in the twin's house.

"Good morning. Can I come in?" Mindy walked in without waiting for a reply.

"Mindy, what do you want?" Trace asked.

"What kind of game are you six playing?" Mindy asked as she watched Amanda spin the globe.

"We are trying to figure out what country to send you to but we can't find one that would take you." Gail said with a smile on her face.

"Mindy, we did not invite you in." Ace said.

"Trace answered." Mindy replied.

"My mistake. I thought that a human being was at the door." Trace remarked.

"I had to come by and ask you all if you have seen today's paper?" Mindy drawled. She didn't wait for a Reply. She pulled out the paper and read "Police officer suspended for taking a civilian's car to chase Robbers that police officer was you Gail."

"I know because I was there. " Gail replied .

"Mindy get out of our house." Trace said angrily.

Mindy started to leave but just before she walked out of the house she said to Amanda "Don't ask for your jobback because I will not give it to you."

"I wasn't planning on asking." Amanda said.

Mindy ran straight into Ariole as she walked out. "Who are you?' She asked. She straightened up her Hair and smiled at him.

"That is our friend Ariole and he isn't interested in you." Ace said.

"Let him make that decision for himself. Would you like to go out with me and get to know me?"

"I don't think so." Ariole replied.

"It is probably better because any friend of theirs are not worth to get to know any way." Mindy said.

"What kind of species are you?" Aroile asked.

"What do you mean what kind of species am I?" Mindy demanded.

"What kind of demon are you?" Ariole asked. Mindy stomped away. The Chosen Ones laughed as she Walked away. "Have you found the charu and the caru yet?"

"Las Angelos California Rock street `112." Amanda replied.

"I will make plan reservations for us." Gail said.

"No need for that." Ariole said as he waved his hand and a circle of light appeared. "Get in. I will take You where you need to go."

CHAPTER 5

"You know I was born and raised in Georgia. I have never left the state. Is the Pacific different from the Atlantic?" Trace wondered.

"That question will not be answered for us because we will not be visiting the ocean." Ace said to Trace.

"Now that you six are here I will be leaving you but don't worry just call my name and I will come back For you." Ariole said.

"Ariole, you only got us to LA. We need to go to 112 Rock Street." Ace reminded him.

"You don't need me for that just take a horse." Ariole replied.

"Why would we want to take a horse?' Ace asked.

"I forgot that traveling isn't done by horses in this time frame. You all will have to take that yellow thing Ariole said.

"Are you referring to a cab?" Ace asked.

"Yes. That is what you call that thing." Ariole said.

"I don't think that one cab can take all of us." Andy said.

"Then you will have to take two cabs." Ariole said as his time circle opened up. Ariole climbed in and he And his time circle disappeared.

They were able to flag down two cabs after Ace pulled two cabs back with his mind because no one was Stopping for them. "You would think that cab drivers would want to stop to make some money."

Andy said.

"May be we look too weird." Trace suggested. The three men got into one cab together and the three Women got into the other cab. The men were in the first cab and the women were behind them. Ace told the cab driver where to go.

Celeste was telling their cab driver the same thing. "Why do you want to go there?" The driver asked.

"To visit a friend." Celeste replied.

"What is your friend's name?" The cab driver asked.

"You do not need to be asking us those questions because it is none of your damn business!" Gail yelled.

The cab driver stopped and looked back at the women. His humane face had disappeared to a grotesque Appearance that resembled a bat. "Gail may be you should apologize to him for yelling at him." Amanda suggested.

"The Chosen Ones will never make it." The demon said. Amanda opened the door on her side and Gail did the same but the doors were slammed shut. "You three can't get out of here." Since Celeste was in the middle she grabbed the demon's head covering up his eyes. The cab started to swerve.

Andy looked back at the cab that the women were in. "There is something wrong with the cab driver that The women are in because he isn't driving straight."

"He must be drunk." Trace said. He had a tight feeling in his chest as he watched the cab swerve.

"Stop the cab! We have to help the women." Ace ordered the cab driver.

"You are crazy to try to stop a drunk!" The cab driver shouted.

"Our girlfriends are in that cab! We have to try and get them out!" Trace yelled.

Ace looked at the driver and moved his hand. The brakes were slammed down. The driver was startled Because he knew that he did not step on the brakes. The gears shifted to park. The driver jumped out yelling That his cab was possessed. The three passengers jumped out of the cab.

"How are we going to stop that cab?" Trace asked his brother.

"I will stop it!" Andy yelled as he levitated himself in the air. He came down on top of the car trying to Block the driver's view hoping that he will stop the cab but it didn't work.

"What is he planning on doing? Ride the cab from the outside?" Trace asked.

"Can you put a car in front of the cab?" Ace asked Trace.

"I can try. What kind of a car?"

"I don't care just stop that cab!" Ace yelled.

Trace visualized and an eighteen wheeler appeared in front of the cab. The cab was going to hit the truck Ace pushed Andy off of the cab before the cab slammed into the truck. "I told you a car not a truck!" Ace said.

"I am sorry but that was the first thing to come to my mind." Trace said. The two men ran towards the Cab. Andy was standing up.

"Are you okay?" Ace asked Andy. Andy nodded as the women jumped out of the cab.

"The driver is a demon!" The women yelled. The demon emerged and headed straight for Trace and Ace Ace moved his hand and knocked the demon down. The demon jumped into the air and came down in front Of Ace's face. The demon yelled and green slime came out of his mouth and all over Ace.

"Yuck! I've been slimmed by a demon!"

"You really do stink." Trace laughed.

"We need our swords!" Gail yelled. They all pictured their swords and the swords appeared in their Hands. Andy jumped into the air and came down knocking the demon down. Celeste did a front handspring And she stabbed the demon in the chest. The demon crumbled to dust.

"I didn't know that you knew gymnastics." Trace said.

"I don't or I didn't think that I did but I guess that I know now." Celeste said. They heard the sound of an engine leaving. They turned around to see that the first cab driver had got back into his cab and had taken off.

"I guess that we are going have to drive the crashed cab." Ace said. The Chosen Ones piled into the cab. The cab was drivable even though there was no windshield. They headed for 112 Rock Street.

CHAPTER 6

"This is it." Amanda said as they climbed out of the cab. They were looking at a two story house that Looked like it belong to a scary movie.

"Are those statues gargoyles looking at us?" Andy asked.

"Yes." Amanda answered.

"Do you have a name for us yet Amanda?" Ace asked.

The door opened before anyone had a chance to knock. A butler was at the door. "Are you here to see Professor Ravasho?"

"Yes." Amanda said.

"Come in." The butler said.

"I do not like the way he said come in." Trace hissed into his brother's ear.

"You never like the way that anyone says anything." Ace remark.

"That isn't true. I like the way Celeste says come here. That is when we are in the bedroom but if she is Mad at me then I don't like the way she says come here."

"I will wait for you all out here." Andy said.

"Come on you big baby." Gail said as she grabbed a hold of his hand and pulled him along.

"Andy is right. Some one should stay out here just in case we don't make it out in a reasonable amount Of time." Trace suggested.

"Okay Andy stay out. If we are not back within thirty minutes then come in after us." Ace commanded.

"I have an idea. Why don't I stay out here with Andy that way if he needs help I can back him up." Trace suggested.

"Okay. You two can stay out." Ace said. Andy and Trace quickly ran back outside.

"I didn't realize that my boyfriend was such a scary cat." Gail remarked. The four Chosen Ones followed The butler. The butler announced the visitors to Professor Ravasho. "What is it you want from me?"

"We would like to know if you recently visited Egypt." Ace required.

"Yes I have. Why do you want to know?"

"We are archeologists and we are interested in Egyptian culture. We would like to know if you found a Bracelet and something that resembles a key with it." Ace required.

"Yes. I did find the artifacts that you have spoken of."

"Can we see them?" Amanda asked.

"How much are you willingly to pay me for them?"

"Nothing. We need those artifacts because when you took them you woke up evil. We need those back To make evil sleep again." Ace explained.

Professor Ravasho pulled out a box. "If you want this you have to pay me for it." Gail ran past the Professor and grabbed the box. The professor only felt the wind. Gail stood beside Ace holding the box. "How did you do that?" The professor was speechless.

"I was on track in high school." Gail opened the box. There was only the caru. "Where is the charu ? Ace demanded.

"I sold it." The professor replied.

"To whom?" Ace asked.

"I don't have to tell you. Now give me my artifact back before I call the police."

"You are going to raise the dead." Ace said.

"I do not believe in curses nor do I believe that the dead will arise!"

"Has thirty minutes passed yet?" Andy asked Trace.

"No." Trace replied.

Andy walked to the back of the house he called for Trace to come back with him to see what he was Seeing. Trace walked back there to see. "Who in his right mind would build a house in a cemetery?" Trace Asked.

"I bet you that people are dying to see this professor." Andy joked.

"Very funny." Trace remarked. Trace screamed along with Andy when hands came out of the graves Grabbing their legs. "Ax." Trace said and an ax appeared. Trace swung chopping the arms that were Holding him then he did the same for Andy.

"Something tells me that the Charuand the caru has been separated." Andy said horrified as they Watched the dead come out of their graves.

"I thought that only the undead will arise." Trace said.

"Apparently the dead will also arise unless these are the undead also." Andy said. Trace took off running. "Trace where are you going? Don't you think we need to stay and fight?" Andy saw them getting Closer so he too turn and ran. He was able to catch up with Trace. Both of them yelled when they were Knocked down onto the ground. Trace looked up to see that the gargoyles had come to life and were the ones To hit them knocking them to the ground.

The two ran to the front door. The door was locked. "Key to the front door." Trace said. A key appeared. He tried to use it but it wouldn't work.

"Trace that is the key to your front door." Andy informed him.

"Key to this house front door." Trace said. Another key appeared and it worked. The two ran inside and Locked the front door. "I guess I have to be specific when I conjure up items." Trace said as they ran off to Find the others.

CHAPTER 7

"Professor, I do not have time to talk to you. Where is the charu?" Ace demanded.

"In the LA museum." Amanda said.

"How do you know that?" The professor demanded.

"Good work Amanda. We need to head to the museum." Ace said, Trace and Andy ran into the room.

"Trace and Andy I know we said to come after us if we were not out within thirty minutes but everything Is alright in here." Ace said.

"Well everything isn't alright out there." Trace said.

"What has happened?" Ace asked but he didn't need an answer because the door was busted down and The dead started to come in.

"The dead has arrived." Trace announced.

"What is going on?" The professor demanded.

"We told you that you have released evil and cause the dead to arise." Ace said as the dead approached.

"Follow me." The professor said. He led them into another room and locked the door behind them. Ace used his mind and pushed a dresser drawer in front of the door.

"Is everything okay professor?" The butler asked.

"Ivan, You will not believe it but the dead is trying to get us." The professor said.

"I believe you in fact all of you are dead." Ivan laughed as his human

25

form took shape to His real form. He was another demon. The same kind that was in the cab.

"Ivan?" The professor said.

"Your butler is really a demon." Ace said.

"Sword." Trace said. All of the Chosen Ones had their sword. Amanda charged and stabbed an undead As they busted in. It had no effect instead the undead grabbed her. She was able to pull free but her shoulder Was bleeding. Celeste was quickly by her side and healed her.

"How do you kill them?" Andy asked.

"We can't kill them because they are already dead. The question should be how do we stop them?" Trace remarked.

The undead approached. Ace pushed them back but they just picked themselves up and kept on coming Ace did it again. "Ace that isn't going to work." Trace said.

"It will buy us some time." Ace grunted as he pushed them back again.

Ivan the demon laughed and said "You can't run. I will kill the Chosen Ones." Gail ran up behind him. She stabbed him through the back. The sword went all the way through. He crumbled to dust.

"Who is laughing now?" Gail said.

"Not us because we still have the undead to deal with." Andy said,.

"Amanda you and I will have to get out of here and get to the museum to find the charu. We will have to Take the caru with us. That is the only way to stop them." Ace said.

"Hello brother dear what about us?" Trace asked.

"Yall will have to stay here and protect the professor." Ace answered.

"Who is going to protect us?" Trace asked.

"I believe that will be our protector's job. Come on Amanda we need to get moving." Ace said as he Pulled her to the window.

"Ace, there is no way to get down from here. It is a long way down. We could get hurt or killed if we try Jumping down. We need some rope but we do not have any." Amanda said.

"Trace get us some rope." Ace ordered.

"Fifty feet rope." The rope appeared in Trace's hands.

"Don't you think this is a little too much rope?" Ace asked.

"Wouldn't you rather have too much rope and not enough?" Trace asked.

"Point well taken." Ace said as he and Amanda started to climb down.

Ace and Amanda made it to the car. Ace pushed some dead back with his mind to get them Away from the car. "You drive Amanda." They only had gone a couple of miles when something hit them From above. "It is the gargoyles how did they come to life?" Ace said. The gargoyles grabbed the vehicle And picked it up into the air. "Jump!" Ace yelled. Both he and Amanda jumped out of the vehicle.

They hit the ground as one of the gargoyles swooped down after them. Ace pushed it back with his mind but It did not stop it. It kept on coming.

"Ace I see some motorcycles parked outside of a diner. Do you think we can use one to escape?"

"We can try." Ace replied as they ran over to one. "No key." Ace said.

They ran inside and saw the motorcyclists. Ace saw a couple of keys laying on the table he took them By using his mind. The keys flew from the table and into his hands. "I hope we have a right key." Ace said As they ran outside.

"This is the right key." Amanda said as she took one of the keys.

"I have never driven a motorcycle before." Ace said.

"I will drive." Amanda said as she started the bike.

"I didn't know that you knew how to drive one of these things." Ace hollered as Amanda drove down The rode.

"I never have driven a motorcycle before but for some reason I know how to operate it just like I knew which was the right key!" Amanda hollered back. They made it to the museum both jumped off and ran to The door. "It is lock!" Amanda yelled. Ace waved his hand and the door opened. They ran inside to look For the charu.

"I see it!" Ace yelled. It was in a glass case. Ace saw a statue by the case he pushed it with his mind Onto the glass case. Glass scattered and alarms started to go off. Ace used his mind and moved the claro to Him. He put the charu and the caru together.

Back at the house the others were running and throwing whatever they could find at the undead. The undead were closing in. "It looks like we are toast!" Andy yelled. All of a sudden the dead turned and Went back to their graves. Everything was quiet.

"I guess that the charo and the claro is back together." Celeste committed.

CHAPTER 8

The police pulled up. "You two stop!" One of the officers shouted at Ace and Amanda.

Ace pushed the police back with his mind then he and Amanda jumped into a police vehicle And took off. "I hope that we do not go to jail for stealing a police car." Amanda said.

"We are not stealing. We are simply borrowing the car. It is for a good cause. We are going to save the World." Ace replied. They parked the car in an empty parking lot then they ran the rest of the way to the Professor's house.

"At least we have lost the gargoyles." Amanda said,.

"We haven't lost them!" Ace yelled as the gargoyles swooped down. They were in the front of the Professor's house. Andy ran out and levitated himself up. He jumped on a gargoyle's back. He used a rope That Trace had conjured up. He tied it around its neck then he jumped onto the other gargoyle and did the Same. The rope was tied together. He then levitated himself off and back onto the ground.

Trace, Celeste, and Gail had a hold of the rope they quickly tied it off to a tree. The gargoyles pulled the Rope tight and when they did they collided with one another and busted into pieces. The Chosen Ones had To jump out of the way of the falling debris.

"We have the charo and the claro." Ace announced.

"I want to take a look at those two items." Andy said as he reached out for the items the charo flew from Ace's hands and clamped down onto Andy's wrist. "Oh hell it chose me."

CHAPTER 9

"Ariole!" Ace yelled.

"You called?" Ariole said as he came out of thin air behind Ace. Ace jumped. "Don't do that!"

"I am sorry if I startled you." Ariole apologized.

"We have the charu and caru. We are ready to go to ancient Egypt." Ace said.

"I want this damn thing off of me!" Andy yelled.

"I see that the charo chosen you Andy. You will just have to keep it on until you have succeeded in Putting Maku back. Follow me." Ariole said as he opened up his time circle and walked into it. The others Followed.

"This is weird." Gail said. Inside the white light visions of time past them. The visions were holographic.

"Look Ace there we are as kids." Trace said excitedly.

"I thought that you told me that you didn't break my skateboard." Ace said.

"I forgot about that but it was an accident." Trace said.

"You owe me a skateboard." Ace said.

"Which World War is this?" Gail asked as the images of the war circled around them.

"World War II." Aroile answered.

"Amelia Earhart." Amanda breathed as she watched her heroin take flight.

"What kind of history is that? I see a Pegasus. That is Greek mythology." Celeste said.

"No. Every thing that is imagined is or at one time was alive." Ariole said.

"Does that mean that dragons were once living?" Andy asked.

"Yes." Ariole answered. Andy screamed as a tyrannosauruses rex appeared. "It appears that I have Traveled back too far back into time."

"Very funny Ariole. I bet you you did that on purpose." Andy accused. Ariole only grinned.

"Ancient Egypt." Amanda breathed as she stepped out of the time circle. Everyone followed. The time Circle closed. "I feel like that I have been here before in fact I feel like it is home." Amanda said.

"It was home to you at one time Amanda." Ariole said.

"Ariole I see people coming. I think that we are going to stand out. Our clothes isn't right." Ace said Ariole waved his hand and everyone found themselves dressed in ancient Egyptian clothing. "Neat." Ace remarked. The people approached and bowed.

"Bow back. It is a sign of respect." Ariole said softly. They all bowed back.

One of the men asked in Egyptian "Do you have some extra water?"

"No. I am sorry." Ace replied back. He was surprised that he could understand and speak Egyptian. When the people passed by Ace exclaimed "Not only can I understand Egyptian but I can also speak it!"

"Why are you surprised? You once lived here not only will you be able to understand the languish but You can also speak it." Ariole explained.

"Where is the City of the Dead?" Ace asked.

"Amanda can tell you that." Ariole answered.

"I don't know where it is at!" Amanda exclaimed.

"Sure you do. All you have to do is use that psychic ability. Psychic energy is all around all you have to Do is to tap into that energy. A psychic can tap into it any time any where just concentrate and tell me the First step we should take." Ariole coached her.

"We need to obtain some camels then go southwest." Amanda said.

Ariole waved his hand and six Camels appeared. Ariole opened up his time circle and climbed in. The circle closed behind him.

"How do we obtain food and water?" Ace hollered.

"Just ask Trace. He can conjure up every thing that you need." Ariole's voice was heard. Ariole was not visible. Ariole laughed then there was only silence.

"I don't think that Ariole is all here." Trace said.

"The man is dead. What do you expect?" Andy asked,

"Amanda lead the way." Ace ordered. The Chosen Ones set off towards the City of the Dead.

CHAPTER 10

"Master, the Chosen Ones are here." A demon said as he bowed down before Maku.

"I know. I felt the time shift when they arrived." Maku said.

"They are here to imprison you again."

"I know that!" Maku yelled. He shot a flame out of his hand hitting the demon causing the demon to scream in pain. "I will not let them imprison me again!" Maku looked at the demon who was still in flames and still screaming. "Oh do shut up." Maku said as he distinguished the fire by shooting water out of the palms of his hands.

The demon bowed as Maku motioned to him to follow. They entered a room which was filled with several types of demons. "Who let the Chosen Ones to come here?" Maku called to the demons. No one answered. "I said who let the Chosen Ones to come here?" Maku repeated loudly. Still no answer. "Some one let them come here." Maku turned to the demon that he had previosly set on fire. He was looking meanly at the demon.

"Please master have mercy on me." The demon begged.

Maku laughed as he flashed his hands at the demon causing the demon to blow up into tiny little fragments. Maku reached his claw hands out and grabbed a small black shadow. It was the soul of the demon. Maku held it at his eyes. The shadow was pleading to him to let him go. Maku shot a green beam from his eyes at the shadow the demon screamed in pain as he started to break up then disappeared it was as if the demon had never exited. All of the remaining demons started to flee in terror Maku laughed as he set several more demons on fire.

CHAPTER 11

Andy yelled as his wrist with the charu on it raised up over his head causing him to loose his balance and he felled to the ground. Andy's wrist was being held up by a force that he couldn't explain. A holographic image came out showing Maku burning demons.

"Who is that?" Trace wondered.

"Maku" Ace replied. Trace glanced at his brother. "I don't know how I know but I do know that that is Maku."

"He is definately mean if he is burning other demons." Celeste committed. The holographic image changed to a pyramid. The pyramid had the sign of the Chosen Ones. "That sign looks like the tattoos on our wrists." Gail observed.

"What does it mean?" Trace asked.

"It is the pyramid we need to go to. It will hold the Crystal triangle." Amanda answered.

"Are you sure?" Ace asked.

"Yes." Amanda answered.

"I think the Charu is showing us the way as well as warning us." Trace said.

"Yeah but it isn't fair that I will die in seven days if we do not defeat Makeo just because the Charu chosen me." Andy complained.

"Don't worry Andy I have a feeling if we can't defeat Maku within seven days we will all die together." Ace said.

"That doesn't make me feel any better." Andy whined.

"It makes me feel bad too." Trace remarked.

Gracu and Ariole were watching the Chosen Ones through a crystal ball. Gracu asked Ariole if the Chosen Ones had any idea on how they died in their past lives in Egypt. Ariole answered no. "'We must not let them know or Makeo could win the battle." Gracu informed Ariole. Ariole bowed and replied "Yes my lord."

"Go and travel with them but do not let them see you. If you are there you can help them faster and do not let Maku reveal to them on how they died." Gracu ordered.

"Yes my lord." Ariole bowed then he entered his time circle and disappeared.

CHAPTER 12

"Sampon where are you?" Maku demanded.

A little gnome like creature came running. He had a big wart on his nose. His small hands were curled. "Yes master."

"I want you to open up the hearth. I need you to pull the lives of the Chosen Ones out."

"But master I hate to interrupt you but the Chosen Ones were killed. You killed them just before you was locked up in the Charu. The fool professor let you out when he dugged the Charu up. He didn't know he had just done. I love mortals they are so stupid." Sampon laughed.

"You are the fool! I did kill the Chosen Ones but that was in ancient Egypt now they are back in the modern world." Maku said.

"They have been reincarnated which means that they wouldn't be the Chosen Ones now." Sampon pointed out.

"They are still the Chosen Ones and they are coming for me. Gracu made sure of that. Their new protector is called Ariole." Maku said.

"Which means that they are coming after you." Sampon said.

"I know that! Open up the hearth now!" Maku screamed.

Sampon went over to a wall and stuck his hand onto the wall. The wallsplit into revealing flames. Screams could be heard coming from the flames. "I have it." Sampon pulled a three D image out of the flames. The hearth closed behind them. The image was that of the Chosen Ones facing off with Maku. Maku took the image and held it on the palms of his hands. He then blew the image off of his hands chanting "Images of my enemy my eyes can see fly to the Chosen Ones seep into their bones open up their minds so that they can see the life that was left behind grasp them by the heart and cause them pain so that they can loose their lives again." The image became a butterfly and floated away to find its target.

CHAPTER 13

The Chosen Ones came into a settlement. There were camels every where. The citizens were walking around. Amanda stood still as she watched a woman grind out something that looked like some type of food. "What is it?" Ace asked Amanda.

"That woman is me." She replied and pointed at the woman.

"She can't be you. You are here." Ace pointed out.

"Look again." Amanda said to Ace. Ace shook his head but when he looked again he had to admit that the woman was Amanda. A man came out and called to the woman "Aretha I need you to come with me." The woman stood up asking the man what is it. The man replied that Maku had stuck again. He said that they needed to get the others." That man is me." Ace whispered to Amanda.

"What are you two looking at? There is nothing here but barren land." Trace said.

"We were watching ourselves in our past lives." Ace answered.

"What are you talking about?" Trace demanded.

"We saw images of ourselves ." Ace said.

"I think the heat is getting to you two because there was nothing there." Trace grumbled as he rode ahead. He hadn't traveled much further when he stopped and watched as a man called to a woman who replied that the camel was giving birth and that she couldn't come right then. The man approached as the mother camel died leaving the baby.

"Trace I see you and me by a dead camel." Celeste said.

"I think the heat is getting to us too because I also see us." Trace replied. The Ace and the Amanda of ancient Egypt approached the two. The ancient Egyptian Ace informed the two that they had to go after Maku now. "Our camel just died we can't leave the baby or it too will die." The ancient Trace said.

The ancient Ace placed a hand onto the ancient Traces shoulder and said. "I know brother but we have to go and stop Maku he is at his weakest if we do not stop him then he will destroy us along with the rest of our nation. The stars are lined up with the moon we should be able to destroy Maku since he is at his weakest.

"Trace and Celeste what is happening?" Ace asked.

"The heat is getting to us because we see ourselves as we were in ancient Egypt." Trace answered.

"Come on you two, you two are only experiencing what Amanda and I have experienced. It is only a vision. We have to keep going to destroy Maku. We do not want him to know that we are here." Ace said.

They hadn't traveled much further when Andy and Gail stopped. They were watching themselves in ancient Egypt. The two were kissing. "Gail are you seeing what I am seeing?" Andy asked. Gail nodded. "You two stop making love and get going . It is time to defeat Maku." The other four Chosen Ones came into the scene. "It is time. The stars are aligned with the moon."

"What are you two seeing?" Ace asked Gail and Andy.

"You four have just come to get us to defeat Maku because the stars are align with the moon." Gail answered.

"That is when he is at his weakest." Andy said.

"Come on lets get moving, it is only a vision and I for one want to destroy Maku and get back to our normal lives in modern times." Ace said. The Chosen Ones pressed forward.

"Gracu it has started. Makeo has opened the hearth. He is showing the Chosen Ones their past lives." Ariole reported.

"I was afraid of that. He is watching them like we are." Gracu said.

"What do we do? We can't let them see their deaths." Ariole said.

"Go as before, stay with them, interfere only if they start to falter." Gracu ordered.

"Yes my lord." Aariole made his custom bow before disappearing in his time circle.

CHAPTER 14

"They are coming closer and they are starting to remember. Yes you all will die again like the first time."

Makeo laughed as he watched the Chosen Ones through the hearth.

The Charu threw Andy's arm up. "Its happening again." This time he was able to maintain his balance and not fall off. They gasped as the holographic images appeared. The image was of them on St. Simon. All of them were on the beach this was the first time that the twins and the women had first met Andy. "Trace stop that!" Andy yelled as Trace put sand down Andy's trunks.

"I am not Trace. I am Ace. You have to learn to tell us apart."

"How? You two are identical." Andy said.

"You just have to hang out with us and find out." Trace said.

"So I am your friend." Andy said.

"Yes we are." The twins said in unison.

"Do you know where I can buy a house? I am living at a motel. I have just been hired at Greystone." Andy informed them.

"You are a lawyer? " Gail smiled the other two women laughed because they know that Gail had found Andy attractive. "I can tell you where one is for rent. I am a police officer. I saw a for rent sign out in front a house the other day."

"Great you can show me where it is at." Andy said. "You five were raised on this island."

"Yes we were. We all have been friends since grade school." Gail answered. "Where are you from?"

"Atlanta. I came down here because I wanted a change besides I am fresh out of law school and Greystone was the only law firm that would hire me."

"You will enjoy it here." Celeste said.

"Yes he will because he has us for friends." Amanda said. Trace had sneaked off and came back with a bucket of water and through it on Andy. Andy yelled "Ace!" Everyone shouted "That is Trace!"

"I think we are being warned." Amanda said as the image of them disappeared.

"Warn about what?" Ace asked.

"I don't know all I can say is that we have better keep our eyes opened." Amanda replied. Gail screamed as the sand exploded in front of them. A huge creature came out of the sand it reminded Gail of an iguana. The camels bolted knocking the Chosen Ones off. "There goes our rides!" Amanda yelled.

"I don't think it is time to worry about the camels. I think we need to worry about this thing." Ace said.

"I hate reptiles." Celeste muttered. The creature turned and came towards Celeste. "I mean I love reptiles." She jumped out of its way as the creature swung its tail.

Andy levated upwards and came down on top of its head. The monster slung him off and then came after Andy. Gail ran in front of Andy "Follow me." Gail took off in a slow motion as the monster came after her. She then took off in high speed.

"Tank." Trace said. A tank appeared and Trace climbed into the tank and took off in the direction that Gail was leading the monster. Trace sited the monster and fired at the monster. Gail was able to get out of the way as the creature exploded. Pieces of the monster started to fall Amanda screamed as a big piece was going to fall on her but Ace pushed it away from her using his power. Trace climbed out of the tank.

"You could have found a better way of killing that thing then conjuring up a tank!" Ace said angrily at his brother.

"I did not see anyone else with an idea besides it worked." Trace shot back.

"You almost killed us with the fallout!" Ace said.

"You kept everyone safe with your powers." Trace argued.

"What are we going to do about the tank? Tanks doesn't exist in this time frame." Ace pointed at the tank as it disappeared.

"Magic hides itself." Trace laughed. A sand storm blew up. "I can't see!" Amanda yelled. Ace shouted for everyone to stay together.

CHAPTER 15

"We are cover in sand and now we are going to die before we can fight Maku." Ace thought as he struggled to come out of the sand. He stopped and began to panic. Sand was caving in on top of him now. He tried to scream but as soon as he opened his mouth sand felled in causing Ace to gag. A wind came up knocking the sand off of the Chosen Ones. "I need a shower." Celeste complained.

"I have sand in my bra!" Gail groaned. She jumped up and down pulling on her bra trying to dislodge the sand.

"I am not telling you where I have sand at." Amanda mumbled.

"I have sand in my underwear and it is driving me crazy!" Trace announced as he was also jumping up and down.

"It doesn't work." Gail informed him.

"I am just going to conjure up a shower for us." Trace said.

"Some how I do not think that even a shower is going to help get all of the sand off of us." Andy grumbled.

"Ace what are you doing? The sand is off of us." Trace said to his brother. Ace was still pushing upward. Fear was in his eyes. Ace collapsed. Trace ran over to him and felt for a pulse. "He has a pulse but it is weak."

Celeste ran over and put her hands on Ace but nothing happened. "I can't heal him!"

"That is because he is no longer with us he is some place else." The five jumped and realized that the voice was Ariole's. He materialized in front of them.

"Have you been with us the whole time?" Gail asked but did not get a response from him.

"He has. He is the one to blow the sand off of us." Amanda realized and answered Gail.

"Guilty as charge." Ariole smiled. Trace put a hand on Ariole's arm and asked him what was happening to Ace. "He thinks he is dying."

"He should have realize by now that we are no longer cover in sand." Trace pointed out.

"Maku is using your past lives as a way to kill yall now." Ariole replied.

"How did we die?" Amanda asked.

"That isn't important." Ariole answered.

Trace grabbed a hold of Ariole and spun him around to face him. "It is if my brother thinks he is dying!"

"Speak to your brother and let him know that you are here and he is safe." Ariole instructed.

"Ace I am here and you are not buried under the sand." Trace grabbed a hold of his brother.

Ace was in another time. He kept seeing the sand coming in all around him and suddenly he was transported to another place. He was inside a pyramid. "We meet again." A voice called out. Ace turned to face the voice. "Maku!" Ace said. Maku's evil laugh echoed off of the walls of the pyramid.

CHAPTER 16

"You do know that you are going to loose this battle like you did the first time." Maku informed Ace.

"We didn't loose the battle. We imprisoned you!" Ace gritted his teeth.

"You only think that you imprisoned me."

"No we did. Who else would have imprisoned you?" Ace asked.

Maku wasn't phased by Ace's words. "The Chosen Ones were so great just the name sent fear through the underworld. You all were the prize for any demon to kill but no one could kill you all except me. I killed you all then and I am going to kill you all again."

"You did not kill us!" Ace yelled as he felt himself being pulled. He was out of the pyramid and standing over him in the desert were the other five and Ariole. Trace hugged his brother. "I thought that I was going to be an only twin." Ace stood up and glared at Ariole. "Did Maku kill us?"

"You do not need to know that." Ariole replied. Ace grabbed a hold of Ariole's shirt. Ace glared at Ariole. "Maku said that he killed us and that he was going to kill us again. Is that true? We need to know so we can be prepare to fight him."

"I am not suppose to tell you but you do have a point and if you would please let go of me I will tell you." Ace let go. "I am sorry but I have to go." Ariole quickly disappeared.

"Ariole get back here! If you were not already dead I would kill you!" Ace shouted.

"My lord, they are wanting to know how Maku killed them. He is planning on killing them the same way as before." Ariole was in his custom bow before Gracu.

"Then go back to the Chosen Ones and let them know." Grace commanded.

"Yes my lord." Ariole replied.

CHAPTER 17

"I should have known not to let go of his shirt." Ace whined.

"There is nothing that you can do about it." Amanda said.

"So Maku really did kill us do you know how?" Trace asked his brother.

"I saw myself suffocating under the sand." Ace answered.

"Ace we really were under the sand." Trace said.

"Yes and that is how I remember being killed." Ace said. "Maku said that he killed us some how I was transported to where he was at. Maku said that he killed us and he will kill us again."

"That is correct he did kill yall the first time but this time I will not it happen." Ariole said as he stood beside them.

"Why did you let it happen the first time?" Trace asked.

"I wasn't your protector then." Ariole answered.

"How did he kill us?" Ace asked.

Ariole glanced at one person to another before he started to speak. "Yall went out to fight him. It was the best time to fight him because the stars were aligned with the moon that is when Maku is at his weakest."

"When is he the strongest?" Ace asked.

"When the moon crosses in front of the sun." Ariole answered.

"During an eclipse." Ace remarked.

"There will be an eclipse at the end of this week. I heard it on the news. I am assuming even though we are in the past that there will still be an eclipse." Gail said.

"Will that be before or after the charu kills me?" Andy asked. "I don't need to know how Maku kills I am assuming the chariot did." Andy smirked.

"Yes Andy you are right the chero chased you then as it does now. You busted into flames because you all did not make the time frame in destroying Maku." Ariole answered.

Andy gulped. "Trace make sure you conjure up a fire extinguisher."

Ariole continued talking. "Gail you was stabbed in the back with a sword."

"But I should have been able to heal her." Celeste interrupted.

"You were the first one to die so you was not able to heal anyone. Maku was able to capture you and lock you up in a esophagus. He released a poisonous gas. Amanda Maku hit you with a lightning bolt. You did not survive."

"I already figured that one out for myself." Amanda interrupted.

"The twins were the last ones to die. You two were twins just like now. You two imprisoned Maku. Trace you was severely wounded in the battle. Ace had to leave you behind to find help. You was able to make a shelter out of a jutted rock you conjured up. Ace was divested to have to leave you behind but there was no way that he could take you with him. He set off into the desert a sandstorm came up. He was suffocated under the sand. It wasn't a natural sandstorm. Sampson Maku's servant caused the sandstorm that took your life."

"Why did you not tell us?" Ace asked.

"That was a past life you didn't need to know but now you do need to know." Ariole answered.

CHAPTER 18

"Ace what are we going to do to keep Makeo from killing us." Andy asked.

"We will just have to meet him on his own terms. I think if we plan it right we can take Maku out on the day of the eclipse." Ace answered.

"Isn't that when he is the most powerful?" Trace asked.

"Yes and he would not be expecting an attack at that time. We were wrong to strike when he is at his weakness. We need to strike when he is at his strongest." Ace replied.

"How do you figure that?" Trace demanded.

"He killed us the first time so we are going to learn from our mistakes and change our attack plans." Ace said.

"Ariole what do you think?" Amanda asked,

"Ace has a point. I think it is wise to attack when Maku least expects it so attack when he is at his strongest he will never expect it." Ariole agreed with Ace. Ariole opened up his time circle. Ace grabbed a hold of Ariole's arm and pleaded with him to stay. "I can't stay. I am not a crusader Yall are the crusaders but I will be there when you need me. I promise you that."

"Sampson!" Maku called. Sampson came running. "In five days I will be at my full powers open up the hearth and let memories come to the Chosen Ones. I will attack and I will kill them just like I did the first time."

CHAPTER 19

"Water I need water! My mouth is so dry." Andy complained. "Your mouth isn't that dry because if it was I wouldn't have to listen to you complain." Trace smirked.

"I am thirsty." Andy repeated.

"Bottle of water." Trace said and a bottle of water appeared in his hands. Trace handed the water to Andy. Andy thanked Trace and Trace said that Andy was welcome.

"Trace I need a Dr.Pepper,a ham and cheese sandwich on rye with mustard mayonnaise lettuce and tomato small bag of sour crème and onion chips and a sneaker bar.' Celeste said.

"What am I! A cashier?" Trace remarked.

"In a matter of speaking you do at times work the cash register at work." Amanda reminded him. Trace produced the food and handed it to Celeste. "Next?'

"I guess we do need a break." Ace said.

"Can we get some shade?" Gail asked and Traced produced a beach umbrella.

"Can we get an air conditioner?" Andy asked.

"No." Trace answered.

"How about a fan?" Andy asked.

"Andy where are you going to plug the fan up?" Ace asked.

"Trace can conjure up electricity." Andy replied.

"I think if I did that then I would get a shock of electricity that would kill me." Trace said.

"Celeste can save you." Andy said.

"I think that we all are trying to take advantage of Trace." Ace said.

"Thank you brother." Trace said.

"You are welcome and by the way I asked for my ham and cheese sandwich to have pickles but you forgot the pickles."

"You can eat your sandwich without pickles Trace glared at his brother. Ace nodded and started to eat. After they finished they continued on their journey.

CHAPTER 20

"Trace can you conjure up a restroom? I really need to go." Celeste whined.

"Go behind a sand dune." Trace replied. "We will not look." Everyone turned around except Trace. Celeste stamped her foot. "I already have seen what you have. We do sleep together." Celeste glared at Trace. He turned around. "Are you done yet?" Trace called after a few minutes.

"Yes." She replied. Everyone turned around in time to see Celeste fall through the sand. Trace called to her but there was no reply. He started to run towards where Celeste had disappeared. Eight arms came out a creature which reminded Trace of an octopus came out of the sand. In one of its arms it held Celeste. "Its crushing me!" She gasped. Ace used his power and pulled the creature's arm that was holding Celeste. She felled free and quickly rolled away from the creature. "What is this thing called a sand octopus?" Celeste wondered.

"It doesn't matter what it is called just run!" Ace shouted .

"You don't have to tell me twice." Andy said as he started to run away.

"Where is Gail?" Ace asked. Everyone were together except Gail.

Andy was slightly ahead of everyone and he called back. "She has already ran off and there is no telling where she is at now!" A blur of sand was stirred up as the sand settled Gail was standing in its place. Andy ran into Gail and felled down. "She is back!" Andy grunted as he still laid flat on his back in the sand.

"Gail I have an idea and I need you for it." Ace announced.

"I am all ears." Gail said. The beast came out of the sand close to them.

"No time to explain just figure it out as we go along!" Ace shouted as he started the sand to spin towards the beast like a tornado.

"Swords!" Trace called and everyone swords appeared in their hands. Ace threw his sword using his mind into the creature. Trace and the women ran up to the creature thrusting their swords into the beast. "Where is Gail? We need her sword in the beast?" Trace called out.

"I have already thrust my sword into the beast. You all are just slow." Gail called out. She was standing by Ace. The others ran by to stand by Ace.

"I guess now it is my turn." Andy said and levitated himself over the creature's head and thrust his sword into the creature's head. The creature screamed asit died. "I do not want to see another sand octopus in my life." Andy grumbled as he landed his feet beside everyone else's.

"Okay everyone we need to keep moving on." Ace told everyone.

"Ariole I know you are watching! We need camels to continue on!" Trace called out.

"Trace why don't you just conjure us up some camels?" Ace asked.

"I keep forgetting that I have that power." Trace admitted an he conjured up the camels.

"Master they keep coming. Every creature that we use against them the Chosen Ones are defeating them." Sampson said.

"It is okay because I will kill them again." Mako said.

CHAPTER 21

"They are very close." Sampson informed Maku. "Are you going wait for them in the pyramid?"

"Yes." Maku answered.

"The Chosen Ones are close to the pyramid." Ariole informed Gracu.

"Good. Ariole go and be with them. I do not need you here by my side watching any more. I need you by the Chosen One's side but don't let them know that you are there. We can't afford to loose them if we do then good doesn't stand a chance against evil if Mako defeats the Chosen One's again. If the Chosen Ones loose then Ariole it will be up to you to stop Maku." Gracu instructed Ariole.

"Yes my lord but my Chosen Ones will not fail." Ariole bowed and left.

"There is the City of the Dead." Amanda pointed.

"I say that it is dead. Nothing is moving and it is all quiet infact it is too quiet. Ace I am scare. Why don't we just call this whole thing off?" Trace said.

"Trace that is a good thought." Andy agreed.

"You two are scary cats." Gail taunted.

"We all are a little scare right now but we have a job and that is to stop Maku." Ace said sternly.

"Gail how can you be so calm?" Celeste asked.

"I am a police officer. We always had to remain calm in a situation if we didn't them we could have been killed. I am a little scare but I am not going to show it." Gail admitted.

"It looks like we are not the only scardy cats." Andy said.

"Come on we need to get down to the city if we don't then we will not be able to defeat Maku." Ace said.

"This is a marvelous place!" Celeste gasped.

"Where is the pyramid?" Ace wondered.

"There." Amanda pointed. The group where no longer on their camels. The camels had been left outside of the city. Ace motioned for everyone to step towards the pyramid and when they did the ground exploded and out came the dead.

"I hate it when the ground explodes! Nothing good ever comes out!" Trace yelled. Ace threw the dead back with a wave of his hand but the dead just came back. "Have you learned nothing? Your powers are useless against the dead!" The chareo caused Andy's hand to raise up and the claro automatically went into the chareo. The dead laid back down and disappeared back into the ground. "I am so glad they are gone." Trace committed.

The Chosen Ones entered the pyramid. They looked around. The charu once again moved Andy's arm. It moved Andy's arm and stopped at a spot inside of the pyramid." Are you looking for this Chosen Ones?" Maku asked. The chareo had stopped at the spot where Maku stood in the pyramid. He was holding the crystal triangle.

"As a matter of fact we are." Ace replied as he used his powers sending the crystal triangle into his hands.

"I do not think that you six have an idea who you all are dealing with." Maku said.

"We know exactly who we are dealing with." Ace challenged.

"I am glad that you do because I haven't a clue!" Trace whispered into his brother's ear. The Chosen Ones were pushed back against the wall of the pyramid and memories started to flood their minds. Maku laughed as the Chosen Ones lay helpless on the floor.

CHAPTER 22

"Help me!" Celeste gasped. She was locked inside an esophagus. Gas was leaking out. She pushed but nothing happened. "Trace! Ace! Andy! Gail! Amanda! Somebody help me!" She became quiet as she felled unconscious.

Gail turned around. "I am coming Celeste!" She started to run but felled as a sharp pain seized her. She realized that a sword had gone through her. She gasped as blood leaked out around her fallen body.

Amanda turned to help Gail but she felt her body jolt as she was thrown up against the wall. She had aburn trail that started at her shoulder and went out at her feet. She had been hit with a lightning bolt which Mako had thrown at her.

Andy levitated himself but before he could come down on a Maku the charu started to smoke before Andy could do something he busted into flames.

"Ace! We are not going to make it!" Trace hollered.

"We will!" Ace hollered back.

"Everyone is dead!" Trace cried out.

"Fight! Our friends will not die in vain!" Ace yelled. Ace's face became pail as he watch blood gush from his brother's throat. A sword had been thrust through Trace's throat. "Trace!" Ace grabbed hold of his brother . He took his shirt off and quickly wrapped it around Trace's throat. He decided if his brother was going to survive then he had to get Trace out. Ace dragged his brother. They had not traveled too far when Trace past out. Ace revived his brother. "You are too weak to travel with me. I need you to make yourself a shade. I am going for help. I will be back. You have my word as your brother."

Trace was able to make a rock like a cliff appear. Ace placed Trace under the rock. Trace looked at his brother but he couldn't speak. "I will not let you die." Ace said. Ace left his brother and went into the desert. Trace watched his brother and knew that he would never see his brother again.

"I have to find help for Trace." Ace mumbled to himself. He climbed back on a camel and took off. Ace thought about his dead friends as he rode. "I must not think about them." The sand started to turn and he felled off of the camal.Ace stood up and tried knock the sand away but the twirling sand became a whirlwind. Sand went down his throat and his nose. Ace couldn't see a thing. He felled and tried to stand back up but couldn't. "Forgive me brother." Darkness felled as Ace was covered up by the sand.

CHAPTER 23

"Sampson, we can go our work here is done." Maku informed Sampson. Mako laughed and said." I told you that I will kill the Choson Ones like the first time."

"No master not like the first time, the first time the twins were able to lock you away." The two started to laugh as they disappeared.

Sand was gently removed from Ace's body. A figure bent down to check on him. "Ace I need you to come back. You are not dead but you will be if you do not respond to me." Ace opened his eyes and saw that Ariole was kneeling beside him. Ace looked around and saw that everyone else were lying on the floor of the pyramid. "You all let Mako play with your minds making you all think that you all were battling him the first time." Ariole walked to Trace's side. "Trace open your eyes. Your throat isn't cut." Trace opened his eyes and saw his brother. Trace smiled as Ace helped him up. "Andy open your eyes."

"No. I do not want to see myself in ashes. I busted into flames." Andy groaned.

"Andy if you were in ashes you would not be able to talk." Ariole said.

"In the afterlife I should be able to talk." Andy mumbled. Ariole pulled Andy up with the wave of his hand. Andy opened his eyes. "I am alive." He said. Ariole replied. "Maku made you think that you busted into flames like the first time."

"Gail it is time to get up. You are not stabbed." Ariole gently shook her and she stood up.

"Why did you pull me up abruptly but you are gentle with her? Gail is a tough woman. She can handle you being rough with her." Andy said.

"I am a gentleman." Ariole replied as he went over to Amanda. He bent down and said." Amanda open your eyes and you will discover that you have no entrance wound or an exit wound from lightning." She did and declared that Ariole must had healed her to which Ariole informed her that it was all in her mind because she let Mako make her believe he had killed her like the first time.

Ariole walked over to Celeste and said. "Celeste time to get up." Celeste sat up and asked." Where is the esophagus I was put in?" Ariole replied that there wasn't one but she only thought there was because that was what Maku wanted her to think.

"You mean to tell us that our own minds were going to kill us?" Celeste asked.

"Yes. The mind is very powerful." Ariole answered.

"Where is Maku now?" Ace asked.

"He is back in the underworld." Ariole answered.

"When is the eclipse?" Ace asked.

"Tomorrow." Ariole answered.

"We will strike Mako tomorrow." Ace announced.

CHAPTER 24

"The eclipse is about to happen and with this crystal triangle I will have full power." Maku laughed as he said that the world will be his.

"Yes master." Sampson said.

The crystal flew from Sampson's hands and landed into Ariole's hands. "I don't think so."

"You can't stop me Ariole. I killed your Chosen Ones. They can't be here to help you." Maku bragged.

"Think again Maku!" Ace yelled as he pushed the demon back using his mind. Ariole disappeared.

"Bring me the crystal pyramid back!" Maku yelled.

"I don't think that Ariole heard you." Ace replied. Sampson started the sand to swirl. Andy levitated into the air and thrust his sword into Sampson's head . Sampson became dust . Maku raised his hand and more demons appeared. The Chosen Ones charged the demons. The demons crumbled to dust as the Chosen Ones drove their swords into the demons. More demons came.

"It is like we kill one demon and get two in its place." Trace grumbled as he thrust his sword into a demon as the demon crumbled to dust three more appeared. "My bad three more takes a demon's place." Mako silently crept off. Ace saw him and ran after him. Maku went to the top of a sand dune.

"I am not going to let you get away." Ace said.

"You are alone. You can't do nothing to me." Maku replied. The eclipse started. "Even as we speak I become stronger." Ace threw Maku with his mind down the sand dune but Maku only glided back up. "You can't hurt me."

The moon had just about covered the sun when Ariole appeared beside Ace. He handed Ace the crystal pyramid." Give that to me!" Maku yelled as he pulled it from Ace's hands using his mind but it never made it to Maku's hands because Ace was able to pull it back to his hands using his mind.

"Raise it up to the sun now." Ariole instructed. Ace did as instructed.

"No!" Maku yelled as Ariole started a chant. "From dust to dust you will return where you will rust in the vanquish land of demons where the evil leaks into veins full of venom is where you will go you will never return back to the flow"

The crystal triangle lit up rays of sunshine filtered through the eclipse . Maku screamed as he became an image. Ariole opened up the crystal pyramid and Maku went into it. Ariole then pulled sand up causing a hole in the desert. He threw the crystal pyramid into the hole and then everything went back to normal. The eclipse was over causing the sun to shine through the sky.

The demons that the other five were fighting turned to dust. They turned around to see Ace standing on the sand dune with Ariole beside him. Ariole took a hold of Ace's hand and all of a sudden the two were standing by the others. "It is over. You all have won the battle." Ariole announced.

.

CHAPTER 25

"Ace do you really think that all of us should be moving in this big house together instead of us living in separate places?" Amanda asked as she surveyed the huge living room.

"This isn't a house this is a mansion!" Celeste exclaimed.

"It is a big house and yes we do need to live together that is if we are going to be fighting demons. We are the Chosen Ones after all." Ace answered Amanda.

"This is an old Victorian house. It has to have a history." Gail said excitedly.

"It gives the house character." Trace admitted.

Andy walked into the house and said. "I just brought a restaurant. I thought that Celeste and Gail could help me."

"Why do we want to leave our old jobs?" Celeste asked.

"I figured that if we had our own business we could leave easier when it came time to fight demons." Andy answered.

"Good point. I will turn in my resignation tomorrow." Celeste agreed.

"Not me I am going over to the police station and tell my sergeant where he can stick his gun and resign on the spot." Gail said.

"Just don't get arrested I am no longer a lawyer." Andy said.

"This is where you six will be living?" Ariole asked as he popped up beside Ace. Ace jumped.

"Yes it is and I would appreciate it if you just don't pop up like that." Ace said through gritted teeth.

"Don't worry I will not be popping in." Ariole said.

"Good." Ace said.

"Which one will be my room?" Ariole asked.

"What did you say?" Ace demanded.

"This house has more than enough rooms. I am your protector so I thought that I should live with yall."

"Where did you stay before us?" Ace asked.

"In my labyrinth all protectors have one."

"I think it would be nice having him here." Amanda said. She hugged him then backed away. "Why are you cold? You have no warmth."

"Because he is the living dead." Ace said.

"It is true. I am dead but I prefer to be call the nonliving dead because that is what I am classified as. There are three classifications. The walking dead which are zombies. The living dead which are vampires and the nonliving dead which are the protectors. We have our physical bodies but we do not have blood circulating. I have no pulse or a heartbeat."

"Are you going to be able to live here with us or should I say be dead here with us?" Ace asked.

"You can say live here after all dying is only the physical. The spirit lives on or in my case so does the body. I am now an immortal instead of a mortal." Ariole informed them.

"You can stay here but we have to get our stuff." Ace said.

"No need to everything is already set up and if you check your bedrooms you will see that I sent the right stuff to the right rooms." Ariole said. The Chosen Ones looked around and the living room were set up. They then went to check out their rooms.

"Ariole how did you know that we were going to choose those rooms for ourselves?" Celeste asked.

"Magic." Ariole answered. "Any one want to go to the beach?"

"Yes but we have to get our swim wear on." Ace said. Ariole snapped his fingers and everyone's clothes were replaced by their swim wear.

"Ariole having you live with us is going to be interesting." Amanda said. Ariole smiles as everyone raced out of the house to the beach which was their back yard.